This Little Tiger book belongs to:

_____

_____

_____

For Nicola, Eliza, Jack and Tom
~ A M

For Miles, with love
~ J M

LITTLE TIGER PRESS
An imprint of Magi Publications
1 The Coda Centre, 189 Munster Road,
London SW6 6AW
www.littletigerpress.com

First published in Great Britain 1995
This edition published 1995

A CIP catalogue record for this book is
available from the British Library

Little Teddy Left Behind

Anne Mangan

Joanne Moss

LITTLE TIGER PRESS
London

Little Teddy woke up and sneezed loudly. Nobody
heard him because no one was there. Nicola and Jack
had moved to a new house.

"I'm all alone," said Teddy. "They've left me behind.
They never were very good at packing. I'm all dusty too,"
he said, and he sneezed and he sneezed.

It grew dark, and at last Teddy went to sleep again . . .

. . . until the next morning when
the cleaning lady's dog spotted him
and picked him up.

"What have you there?" asked the
lady, and when she saw how grubby
Teddy was, she grabbed him with
her big hands . . .

. . . and popped him into the washing machine!

"Oh help!" cried Little Teddy, but nobody heard his tiny squeak.

It was dreadful in the washing machine. Teddy was whirled round and round until he was quite dizzy. He growled his very loudest growl, but nobody came to rescue him.

At last he was spun dry and the machine stopped. Teddy lay there among all the damp clothes, wondering what would happen next.

The cleaning lady opened the machine door and
took out Teddy. "You're not quite dry yet," she said.

"I am so!" growled Little Teddy, but she took no
notice and pinned him upside-down on a clothesline.

"I'd rather be dirty and the right way up!" he
cried, but of course nobody heard his tiny squeak.

It was windy and
Teddy swung back
and forth on the clothesline.
It was exciting in a way, like flying in space.

All at once the line broke, and Teddy fell down, down,
down into the grass. Butterflies flew all around him and
bees buzzed over his head. Teddy liked the bright cheerful
butterflies, but he was a bit afraid of the bees.

"You scare me," he squeaked, but the bees were too
busy to hear him.

Suddenly Teddy felt hot breath in his ear.

"Oh no!" he cried. "It's that dog again!"

The dog seized the little bear in his big teeth
and pushed through a very prickly hedge into the
next garden.

"Oh, my poor fur!" gasped Teddy.

A lady looked up as the dog rushed on to her lawn.
"Ugh, he's got a rat in his mouth!" she screamed and
threw a gardening glove at them.

"I'm not a rat!" growled Teddy.

The dog ran out through the garden gate into a wood.

"Oh, I do wish he'd drop me," thought Teddy
and at last he did. The dog spotted a rabbit and ran off,
leaving Teddy behind.

Teddy lay very still, hoping the dog wouldn't come back.
It was quiet in the wood – but not for long. Two children
came rushing towards him.

"Hey, a little teddy!" cried one of the children.

"That's me," thought Teddy. "Now what?"

He soon found out.

"Catch!" the boy yelled and poor Teddy
was tossed from one to the other until he felt quite
sick. Jack and Nicola had never played with him like this.

At last the children grew tired of their game and the
girl flung Little Teddy high into the air.

Up, up, up he sailed, right into the branches of a tall
tree. No sooner had he landed than he heard an angry
chittering noise.

"Trying to steal my nuts, are you?"

Teddy looked down. At the end of his branch a squirrel was glaring at him. Teddy tried to explain about the boy and girl and their awful game of catch, but the squirrel didn't seem to hear. "This is my tree!" he said, giving Teddy a sudden push. The little bear fell down, down, down . . .

. . . and landed on a wooden floor.

He was lying there, getting his breath
back and worrying whether Jack and Nicola
would ever find him again, when he heard
children's voices. He tried his growl and he
tried his squeak, but they were too small for
the children to hear him.

The floor was as dusty as the empty room
he had left behind. Once again Little Teddy
began to sneeze and sneeze. The sneezes were
louder than the growl and the squeak, and at
last the voices came nearer . . .

"Look, there's a ladder!"

"It's a tree house!"

Two faces were peering at him – two faces he knew very well!

"It's Little Teddy!" cried Jack. "How did he get into our new garden? I thought he was all packed up."

"I don't know, but it doesn't matter," said Nicola, giving Teddy a hug. "We've found Teddy *and* a tree house."

"It's Teddy's tree house," said Jack. "He found it."

His very own house! Little Teddy liked the idea.

A few days later Nicola and Jack had
a housewarming party for all their friends.
Each friend brought a teddy bear, so that Little Teddy
could have his own friends at his own housewarming
in his new home in the big tree.

More exciting adventures from Little Tiger Press

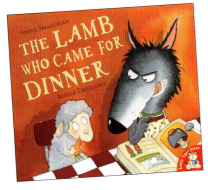

THE LAMB WHO CAME FOR DINNER
STEVE SMALLMAN
JOELLE DREIDEMY

MEGGIE MOON
ELIZABETH BAGULEY
illustrated by GREGOIRE MABIRE

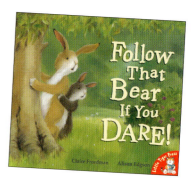

Follow That Bear If You DARE!
Claire Freedman   Alison Edgson

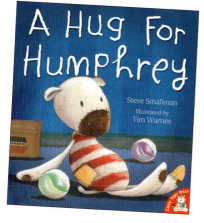

A Hug For Humphrey
Steve Smallman
Illustrated by Tim Warnes

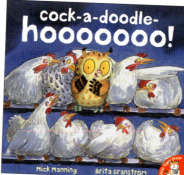

cock-a-doodle-hoooooooo!
Mick Manning   Brita Granström

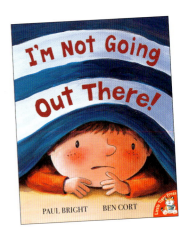

I'm Not Going Out There!
PAUL BRIGHT   BEN CORT

For information regarding any of the above titles
or for our catalogue, please contact us:
Little Tiger Press, 1 The Coda Centre,
189 Munster Road, London SW6 6AW
Tel: 020 7385 6333 Fax: 020 7385 7333
E-mail: info@littletiger.co.uk
www.littletigerpress.com

Little Teddy wakes up one morning
to find that Jack and Nicola, his owners,
have moved away and forgotten to take
him. So begins an incredible series of
adventures for Little Teddy. Will he
ever find Jack and Nicola again?

ISBN 978-1-85430-125-3

9 781854 301253

90200>

£4.99

www.littletigerpress.com